D1532773

When a child gets this book, Muscle Man gets his chicken wings.

CARTOON NETWORK BOOKS
Penguin Young Readers Group
An Imprint of Penguin Random House LLC

Penguin supports copyright. Copyright fuels creativity, encourages diverse voices, promotes free speech, and creates a vibrant culture.
Thank you for buying an authorized edition of this book and for complying with copyright laws by not reproducing, scanning,
or distributing any part of it in any form without permission. You are supporting writers and allowing Penguin to continue to publish books for every reader.

CARTOON NETWORK, the Logos, REGULAR SHOW, and all related characters and elements
are trademarks of and © Cartoon Network. (s15) All rights reserved. Published in 2015 by Cartoon Network Books, an imprint of Penguin Random House LLC,
345 Hudson Street, New York, New York 10014.
Manufactured in China.

ISBN 978-0-8431-8313-9 · 10 9 8 7 6 5 4 3 2 1

REGULAR SHOW

"IT'S A REGULAR LIFE"

CARTOON NETWORK BOOKS

An Imprint of Penguin Random House

Christmas Eve had arrived, and snowflakes filled the air. The Park was abuzz with busyness! And no one was busier than Skips. But things were getting out of hand. They were not going well. Not very well at all . . .

In fact, things were going very, very, *very* . . .

. . . BADLY!
The lights were all tangled, and the snow was too deep.
It was all Skips could do on this cold, snowy eve . . .

. . . to keep from crying.

The more Skips helped, the worse things became. He simply could do nothing right! But worse than the jumbled lights, worse than the snow-covered paths, worse than the dinky decorations—worse than *everything*—was the snowman . . .

The snowman he wanted was the greatest and grandest, something unreal,
the most *snowmanliest*. But *this* snowman was a disaster.
And everyone from rival East Pines Park was watching . . .

And just when Skips thought Christmas Eve couldn't get any worse, a horrible *RUMBLE* shook the earth.

The snowman collapsed to the ground!

Skips gasped with disgust and stared at the mess all around.

Skips's heart was heavy, his spirit sad. Christmas in the Park would be ruined. And it was all his fault . . .

"I'm useless!" Skips cried out. "The Park would be better off without me!" Full of dismay, Skips *skipped away!*

His friends watched him go. They looked to the clouds and shouted, "Please, *somebody*, HELP OUR FRIEND SKIPS!"

Skips skipped across the Park and stopped beneath the towering metal gate. He would leave. He would never come back. He decided right then, with a stern yeti look. He would never return to the Park again . . .

"I wish I'd never worked at the Park," Skips said, and he took a slow, heavy skip forward. Little did he know that crazy Christmas magic was in the air, doing crazy Christmas things . . .

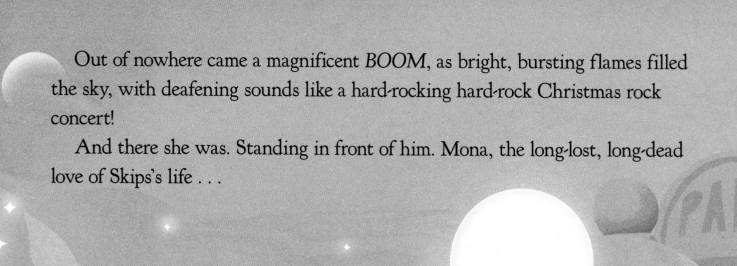

Out of nowhere came a magnificent *BOOM*, as bright, bursting flames filled the sky, with deafening sounds like a hard-rocking hard-rock Christmas rock concert!

And there she was. Standing in front of him. Mona, the long-lost, long-dead love of Skips's life . . .

Mona! My deceased darling! Can it be?

Mona smiled. "Skips, my love, I am your guardian angel!"

Guardian angel? Mona, my love, I miss you so much. But where, my love, are your wings?

I will earn my wings, you'll see, by granting YOUR wish.

Skips was befuddled.

"You wished you'd never worked at the Park," Mona said. "And as of THIS INSTANT, my dearest, you *never have!*"

And as she spoke, Skips heard strange sounds coming from the Park—sounds unlike any he'd heard before. Dings and whistles and screeches and bangs.

Skips's heart pounded as he turned and saw . . .

"The Park is all wrong!" Skips exclaimed. "This doesn't make sense . . ."
Skips raced to Pops's aid, chasing the bullies away. "Scram!" Skips shouted.
And they scattered and pattered like mice.

Pops smiled. "Jolly good show, kind stranger. An impeccably timed rescue!"

"Pops!" Skips said. "It's me, Skips!"

"I'm afraid I don't know anyone by that name," Pops said, turning
and walking away. "We have never been introduced."

"Then travel we must," Mona said. And away they sped, hand in hand,
to see what else had changed . . .

As they arrived at his garage, his heart sank lower than it
had ever sunk before. Muscle Man clearly lived there now!

Popping his head out the door, Muscle Man shouted, "Hey, bro, you better BEAT IT
before you get BEAT UP. And you know who will do the beating?"

"Let me guess," Skips said. "Your mom?"

"MY MOM!" Muscle Man shouted. "Hey, wait, how did you know I was going to say that?"

But Skips didn't move as Muscle Man charged.

There was a **PA-POW** and a muscly Muscle Man punch, and Skips tumbled through the air and crashed down into the snow.

"Mona." He looked up.

"What's happening?"

I told you, my love. I've granted your wish—this is what the Park would be like if you'd never worked here.

But it's such a mess! And Muscle Man is a *real* jerk now!

Skips wouldn't believe it. He couldn't! "NO! THIS IS TOO WEIRD!" he exclaimed.

"I want to see Mordecai and Rigby! They'll know what's going on!"

With that, Skips and Mona set off to find Mordecai and Rigby.

Skips balled up his fists very tight and said, "I need to speak with Benson. He'll straighten out this mess."

But Benson wasn't in charge at all! He was sweeping the floors like poor old Cinderella! And towering over him was Gene!

"Benson!" Skips exclaimed. "Why aren't you running the Park?! What's Gene doing here?"

Benson? Run the Park? HA! This park is MINE! All the parks are mine!

"But, Benson, I know you! We're friends!" Skips proclaimed.

Benson hung his head and said, "I have *no idea* who you are. I haven't managed the Park for years, and I don't like you teasing me about it. Now get out of here! I need to finish sweeping so Gene will feed me."

She planted a big smooch on Skips's lips, and magically everything changed . . .

Mordecai and Rigby shook Skips from what must have been a dream, and he finally opened his eyes.

"Skips!" Mordecai said. "Are you okay?"

"Wait," Skips said. "What did you call me? Did you call me Skips? YOU KNOW MY NAME?!"

Rigby said, "Duh! You're Skips! You do stuff. You know, so Mordecai and I don't have to . . ."

Mordecai slapped Skips on the back. "The Park would fall apart without you, Skips. We'd probably *all* fall apart without you."

Skips was so happy, he could hardly believe it. He leapt to his feet, and then, with a great smile on his face . . .

He skipped! He skipped like he had never skipped before! "I'm back! I'm back! Mordecai, Rigby, Benson, Pops, Muscle Man, Hi-Five Ghost—*everyone*— it's Christmas Eve, and I'm home, and it's *great!*"

Skips skipped toward his disastrous snowman.
And what he saw made his eyes go wide.

We finished the snowman, Skips.
We made some changes. We modeled
it after someone we know. Someone
we respect, admire, and think is
just really great . . .

Skips grinned and looked to the sky. The snowman made him happy. But one thing made him even *happier*: Mona, the love of his life, his angel, had *definitely* earned her wings.

THE END